# A THING CALLED SNOW

Dedicated to
the wild

**OXFORD**
UNIVERSITY PRESS

Great Clarendon Street, Oxford OX2 6DP

Oxford University Press is a department of the University of Oxford.
It furthers the University's objective of excellence in research, scholarship,
and education by publishing worldwide. Oxford is a registered trade mark of
Oxford University Press in the UK and in certain other countries

Text and illustrations copyright © Yuval Zommer 2020

Author photo by Ian Hessenberg

The moral rights of the author and illustrator have been asserted
Database right Oxford University Press (maker)

First published 2020

British Library Cataloguing in Publication Data
Data available

ISBN: 978-0-19-276982-4

1 3 5 7 9 10 8 6 4 2

Printed in China

Paper used in the production of this book
is a natural, recyclable product made from wood
grown in sustainable forests. The manufacturing process conforms
to the environmental regulations of the country of origin.

# A THING CALLED SNOW

YUVAL ZOMMER

OXFORD
UNIVERSITY PRESS

Fox and Hare were born in the spring,
grew up in the summer, and were
best of friends by autumn.

Fox liked to jump, leap, and bounce and was very good at sniffing far away things.

Hare liked to bounce, leap, and jump and was very good at **hearing** far away things.

Then one day Fox's nose **twitched**.
Hare's ears **pricked** . . .

'Winter is on its way,' said Tern. 'I'm flying south, but soon you will be able to jump, leap, and bounce in this thing called snow!'

But what exactly was snow?

Before Fox and Hare could find out, Tern had already gone.

They decided to venture into
the great forest to ask Bear.

'What is snow like?' they said.

'Snow is white, like your fur,' said Bear.

So they thanked Bear and set off looking
for something as white as their fur.

At the forest's edge they found Caribou, who was nibbling something white among the grasses.

'Excuse me,' said Hare. **'Is that snow?'**

'No, these are flowers,' said Caribou.
'Snow is COLD, like your noses.'

So they thanked Caribou and bounded
across the meadow, looking for
something as cold as their noses.

'Hello, there,' called Fox.
'Is that snow?'

So they followed the stream, searching
for something as fluffy as their tails.

Round a rocky bend, they found Salmon,
leaping through an icy stream, flashing bright.

'No, this is spray,' said Salmon.
'Snow is fluffy, like your tails.'

Hare heard a honk and looked up at the great sky.

'Is that snow?' he called to Goose, who was flying overhead.

'No, these are clouds,' said Goose.
'Snow is **sparkly**, like your eyes.'

Fox and Hare were now getting
too tired and cold to search
for this thing called snow.

And it was starting
to get dark.

So they stopped by
the edge of a lake.

'Snow?'
whispered Fox.

The inky water
shimmered with
something sparkly.

'Stars,' yawned Hare, 'which means it's our bedtime.'

But they were too far away to get home before dark.

'Let's sleep here tonight,'
said Fox. 'We'll find our way
back in the morning.'

And she wrapped her thick
tail around them both.

Curled up together for warmth,
Fox and Hare soon fell asleep.

They didn't see the white,

cold,

fluffy,

sparkly

flakes

that started to fall

softly from the sky.

They didn't hear Bear and Caribou crunching
through the snow to look for them.

Hare and Fox woke up to a bright,
white morning like no other.

'Hello,
snow . . .

'Hello, snow!
Hello, snow!'
they squealed.

'Hello, Bear! Hello, Caribou!' they yelped,
as they jumped, leapt, and bounced in the
whitest, coldest, fluffiest, sparkliest snow.

'We're so glad we found you!' said Bear.
'We were worried you were lost.'

'Now let's find our way
home,' said Caribou.

'Follow us!' said
Hare and Fox,

who remembered every step
they had taken around the lake,

across the meadow,

along the stream,

through the forest . . .

. . . and they were followed by a thing called snow.